THE
ACCUSATION

by Anne Schraff

D1372595

Perfection Learning® Corporation
Logan, Iowa 51546

Cover Design: Mark Hagenberg

Cover Image Credit: Photodisc Royalty-free

For information, contact:
Perfection Learning® Corporation
1000 North Second Avenue, P.O. Box 500,
Logan, Iowa 51546-0500.
Tel: 1-800-831-4190 • Fax: 1-800-543-2745
perfectionlearning.com

Paperback ISBN 0-7891-6657-7
Reinforced Library Binding ISBN 0-7569-4740-5

2 3 4 5 6 PP 09 08 07 06

1 OSCAR QUINTERO, a junior at Pico High School, had always had plenty of friends. He couldn't remember a time when he wasn't organizing a baseball game, setting up homemade ramps for skateboarding, or just hanging with his friends. Oscar's teachers all liked him, except for one—Philip Meeker, who taught English. Oscar had known from the first day he walked in to Mr. Meeker's room that the teacher did not like him, but he couldn't understand why.

"Oscar Quintero," Mr. Meeker had said on the first day, "would you mind choosing a seat closer to the front of the room? I'm a bit leery of students who scramble to the back. They are usually the same students who waste class time reading magazines hidden in their binders."

Mr. Meeker was smirking as he spoke. He hadn't even known Oscar then. Oscar wasn't at all what Mr. Meeker was implying. Oscar was a great student. He would be the first in his family to finish high school. He expected to be the first to go to college too. He was proud of his 3.98 grade point average. He resented Mr. Meeker's snide attitude.

And after that, it only got worse. Oscar believed the teacher was constantly singling him out for harassment. It was the third week of school, and Oscar was having lunch with his friends, Tina Asaro and Danny Silva. Oscar talked about Mr. Meeker's attitude toward him.

"He's just got it in for me," Oscar complained. "At first I thought I might be imagining things, but he's like a cat sitting outside a mouse hole waiting for the poor rodent to appear so he can pounce on him. Meeker has a sixth sense. He seems to know when I haven't done every bit of the homework, and that's when he attacks."

"Nobody likes Meeker," Danny said. "He's not just picking on you, dude. He picks on everybody."

Danny was not a good student. He was barely scraping by with a D. He stood a good chance of not getting his high school diploma, and he didn't really care.

"Oscar, just read everything that's assigned, and then Mr. Meeker won't have a leg to stand on," Tina said.

Tina tossed her silky black hair impatiently. She didn't like whining. Both her parents were college teachers. She was an excellent student.

"Tina," Oscar said, "you've got to admit he zeroes in on me more than on anybody else. Like today, when we were talking about the guy in the story about the piece of string. Meeker kept correcting the way I pronounced Maitre Hauchecorne . . . like anybody could get that right the first time!"

"Just chill, Oscar," Tina said. "Do your best and forget about that teacher. My mom is always telling me that the only person who can hurt you is your own self!"

"I don't know about that," Danny laughed. "A guy who has it in for me and gives me a good left jab can do me a lot of harm!"

....

That evening everyone in Mr. Meeker's English class had to write a one-paragraph statement about the moral of the story

"The Piece of String." Oscar reread the story so he would be sure to get it right. He was determined not to give Mr. Meeker any excuse to cut him down again.

The story line of "The Piece of String" was pretty simple. A common man, Maitre Hauchecorne, picked up a string he found lying in the dirt because he thought it may be useful to him someday. An enemy saw him bend down to pick something up, so when a black pocketbook turned up missing, the enemy accused Hauchecorne of stealing the item. Hauchecorne frantically pleaded his innocence. However, even when somebody turned in the pocketbook, everyone in the village still believed Hauchecorne was somehow involved in the crime. In the end the poor man died of a broken heart.

Oscar began his paragraph: Sometimes there is no way to defend yourself when you are wrongly accused of a crime.

....

The next day Oscar confidently put his paper on Mr. Meeker's desk. But his confidence did not last long.

Mr. Meeker thumbed through the papers as if he were looking for one paper in particular. Then he said, "There is a striking similarity to most of these, as if too much consultation took place. I wanted your original ideas." He paused then, his gaze raking the class and eventually focusing on Oscar. "Now, here's a brilliant sentence that required a lot of thought. 'Sometimes there is no way to defend yourself when you are wrongly accused of a crime.' Well, duh!"

Oscar felt his skin tingling with rage. Mr. Meeker was doing it to him again! What was his problem? Why couldn't he get off Oscar's case? What was it about Oscar that turned the teacher into such an unfair creep?

Philip Meeker was a reed-thin little man who always wore pinstriped shirts and pressed slacks. His ties were always the same color as the pinstripes. He was about 5 feet 6 inches tall and likely he did not weigh more than 140. He was the classic weakling who was targeted by beefier bullies.

Maybe that was it, Oscar thought. Oscar

was a big, well-built kid. He was only 16 and already over 6 feet tall, and he weighed in at 170. He was a linebacker with the Pico Panthers, the school's football team. Maybe Oscar reminded the teacher of his own miserable high school years when he was the object of abuse by the big jocks. But that wasn't Oscar's fault. He'd had nothing to do with Mr. Meeker's bad experiences. And he didn't want to take the fall for them.

After the rest of the students had filed out at the end of the period, Oscar walked up to Mr. Meeker's desk. "Can I have a word with you, Mr. Meeker?"

"I suppose you can because you're standing in front of my desk right now. But what you should have said is *may* I have a word with you?" Mr. Meeker said. "That would be correct English. So, what do you want to talk about, Oscar?"

"I get the feeling that there's something about me that bothers you, Mr. Meeker. If so, then maybe we should talk about it," Oscar said.

"Bothers me?" Mr. Meeker said smiling snidely. "What an interesting comment.

I'm not bothered by anybody actually. I am bothered by behavior. When I see a student who isn't working up to his capabilities, I'm bothered. When I meet a lazy student who would prefer standing around gossiping instead of studying, I'm bothered. Do you get the picture?"

"Look," Oscar said, trying to control his temper. "I'm a pretty good student. If you don't believe that, look at my record. I make good grades, and I'm proud of them. So I don't see why you're always on my case."

Mr. Meeker leaned back in his chair and put his hands behind his head. "Do you know the word *paranoia*?" he asked.

"Yeah, but that's not what's going on here," Oscar said. "I'm not just imagining that you have no use for me. I know you have a problem with me, and I'd just like to find out what it is so we can straighten it out."

"No problem here. You just do your work, and we'll get along," Mr. Meeker said. "Spend more time studying and less time hanging out gabbing with your friends."

Oscar turned and left the room, angrier than ever. Mr. Meeker knew exactly what Oscar was talking about, but he wouldn't admit it.

Oscar lived in an apartment with his mother near Pico High School. His mom was divorced, and Oscar was the youngest of four children. His three older sisters were all married now. None of them had finished high school. According to his mom, they had all married too young and now they were struggling.

Oscar's mother had not finished high school either. She had been just 17 when she married, and her husband was a restless man. When Oscar and his sisters were young, their dad left, and now he returned at infrequent times, usually bearing gifts and money, trying in those brief visits to be a father again.

"You're the smart one in the family, Oscar," his mom would often say. "You are going to get a good education and amount to something important. Then you can marry and give your family a good life. Everybody else in this family did it backward—forget school, party all the time, get married, and then try to figure out how to support the family."

But now Oscar was worried as he had never been before. What if Mr. Meeker managed to upset all his plans? What if he flunked Oscar and brought his precious grade point average down? Oscar felt angry and frustrated, and he shared his feelings with Danny after school.

"Did you see Meeker?" Danny asked.

"Yeah, and it was a big waste of time," Oscar said bitterly. "He played me for a fool, a *bobo*. He acts like he hasn't got a problem with me, but, Danny, he hates me! I can see it every time he looks at me."

"Maybe he doesn't like Mexicans," Danny said.

"No, that's not it. He likes Tina and Anna Maria and Carlos. He's always laughing and joking with them," Oscar said.

Danny shrugged. "Well, *hermano*, maybe he's just a mean dude who hates jocks. Maybe his life isn't so good, and he's got to hate somebody. Maybe his wife nags him or he's got kids who're driving him crazy. Maybe he's a frustrated jock himself who never had the body or the talent for it, and he hates guys like you who're good athletes. Or maybe he's just nuts. Who knows?" he said.

When Oscar got home, his mother was still at work. She had struggled for a long time to raise her children alone while taking health-care courses. She had finished her education and was now a certified nursing assistant. She always said that if she had been smart as a girl, she would have postponed dating and marriage and gotten her degree as a registered nurse. She would be making twice the money now at least.

Oscar started dinner as he always did when his mom was working late. He cut up the salad and put the casserole in the oven. Then the phone rang.

"Oscar," Tina cried excitedly, "did you hear about Mr. Meeker?"

"No, what?" Oscar asked.

"He was attacked at Pico—in the parking lot! He was beaten really badly. They took him to the hospital. He's in the emergency room. Somebody at school saw him, and he was all bloody, and oh, it was awful! He looked like he was dying or something," Tina said.

Oscar got numb. He didn't like Philip Meeker. In fact, he hated him. But still, this was shocking and terrible. And Oscar was afraid somebody might think he did it!

2 OH MAN, Oscar thought to himself, somebody else must hate Meeker even more than I do. Or maybe it was a robbery—some doper looking for drug money. Or a carjacking that turned violent.

His mom came home more than an hour late. She had been near the emergency room when Mr. Meeker was brought in. "Everybody was running around trying to help him," she told Oscar. "Your English teacher, Oscar! I couldn't believe it! What is wrong with this world? A teacher is walking to his car in a school parking lot, and he is attacked like that!"

"Do they think he's going to . . . you know, live?" Oscar asked nervously.

"Oh, I don't know, Oscar," his mom said. "The doctors and the ER nursing staff were caring for him. I'm just a CNA." His mom often put herself down like that. She was so embarrassed that she was not a registered nurse.

Oscar had never talked to his mother about his problems with Mr. Meeker. He figured his mom had enough to deal with trying to make ends meet and help her daughters and grandchildren. She didn't need to be burdened with Oscar's school problems.

"I suppose it was a robbery," Oscar said. "It was getting dark, and some thief just saw this lone guy going to his car."

"This is not a bad neighborhood," his mom said as she carried the casserole to the table. "Sure, there are gangs, but it's been better lately. I don't see as much graffiti. We haven't had a drive-by shooting in a long time. Things are getting better—and now this! A teacher brutally attacked on the campus of our high school!"

Oscar always enjoyed his mom's cooking, but tonight he had a hard time eating. He felt nervous about what had happened. So many students heard him sounding off about Mr. Meeker. What if the police found out? In cases like this, the police questioned everybody, and if several people mentioned that Oscar

Quintero was having problems with Mr. Meeker, the finger of suspicion would point to Oscar.

Danny called later while Oscar was working on his math. "Hey, man, you heard, huh?" he said.

"Yeah, Tina called me, and my mom was working at the hospital when they brought Meeker in," Oscar said.

"Well, no tears from us, eh, *hermano*?" Danny said.

"Look, Danny, I'm not celebrating any guy getting his head smashed like that," Oscar said. "Yeah, he wasn't being fair with me, but I'm not going to sink so low that I'm glad he's over there in the ER now."

"Yeah, sure, I hear you," Danny said, "but just the same, better him than somebody like Mr. Dunphy. Everybody likes Dunphy."

Ed Dunphy taught American history. He was a young black man who laughed and joked with his students but demanded a lot from them. He was fair and interesting.

"Anyway," Oscar said, "I hope the guy is okay."

"I wonder who did it, though. A couple of guys were there right after it happened. They said Meeker was lying face down on the blacktop, and his wallet was bulging from his back pocket," Danny said.

A fresh chill went through Oscar's body. Not a robbery? If the wallet was left, the motive could not have been money. A man savagely beaten like that for no reason? "Maybe, uh . . . it was a robbery or a carjacking gone sour . . . like maybe Mr. Meeker resisted and then the guy heard other people running and he fled without the money," Oscar speculated.

Danny laughed. "*Hermano*, did you say *carjacking*? Are you forgetting what kind of wheels Meeker has? A beat-up old Chevy with two crinkled fenders?" he said.

"So what do you think happened?" Oscar said.

"Somebody who didn't like him went over the edge, dude," Danny said. "It was an act of hate. That's how it looks to me. They did too much damage for it to be anything else."

"Well, I didn't like the guy, but I can't

imagine busting his head like that," Oscar said.

After the phone call with Danny, Oscar felt even worse. He found it hard to sleep that night. He kept dreaming about Meeker in his pinstriped shirts and brightly colored ties. All during the dreams, Meeker was smirking at Oscar, saying with his superior look, "Look, punk, I'm the teacher and this is my classroom, and I can do anything I want."

Then Oscar dreamed about poor Maitre Hauchecorne from "The Piece of String." Could an innocent man really be destroyed by false accusations?

....

Oscar was not surprised when he was called from class the next morning to talk to a police officer. He went to the principal's office where Ms. Hopkins had set up an interview room for the police.

The detective was a dark-skinned Hispanic, Sergeant Jim Velez. "So," he consulted his notebook, "you are Oscar Quintero, one of Mr. Meeker's students."

"Yeah, period 1 English," Oscar said.

He didn't want to appear nervous and further arouse suspicion. Oscar had read once about a man who was arrested for a brutal murder just because he sweat profusely when first interviewed by the police. Of course they'd found other evidence, but the nervous demeanor had led to further scrutiny of the man. Oscar felt like his insides were shaking, but he tried to seem calm.

"I understand you had some problems with Mr. Meeker?" Velez asked, looking right at Oscar. He had little black eyes, sharp and bright like a bird's eyes.

"I was doing okay in English, but Meeker seemed to have something against me, you know. My friends told me Meeker picked on everybody, and I guess that's so. Maybe I was being sensitive or something," Oscar said, trying to minimize his problems with Mr. Meeker. Oscar fidgeted in his chair, and Velez seemed to notice that. He didn't miss much.

"Several kids overheard you yesterday saying you were going to have it out with Mr. Meeker," Velez said.

"Yeah, I talked to him, and we worked it

all out. We understood each other better, I think," Oscar lied.

Sergeant Velez scribbled something on his pad. Oscar worried that some kids might remember Oscar saying the meeting was a waste of time. Then Velez would know Oscar was lying . . . and he'd be in even more trouble.

"So," Velez said in his cool, professional voice, "you left the school campus yesterday at what time?"

"Uh, 3:30 like usual except when there's football practice," Oscar said.

"How do you get home from school?" Velez said.

"I walk. Me and my friend Danny Silva walk together most of the way, then he turns off. Then I go to our apartment," Oscar said.

"How far from the school are you and how long does it take to walk?" Velez kept jotting things on his pad.

"It's uh . . . less than a mile. It usually takes 10 or 15 minutes," Oscar said. "Unless I'm jogging. Then it's much quicker."

"So, was anybody home when you got there?" Velez asked.

"No. My mom's a nurse, and she works different shifts. She got home pretty late yesterday," Oscar said. He knew he had a problem right here. He was all alone from around 3:45 to 7:00. He could have easily gone back to school, attacked Mr. Meeker, and then returned home. Based on Tina's phone call, Oscar figured Mr. Meeker was attacked around 4:45 or 5:00. That gave Oscar a huge window of opportunity, a long span of time when he had no alibi.

"Well, we'll probably want to talk to you some more," Velez said. "But that's all for now. You can go back to class."

"Uh, will he . . . Mr. Meeker be okay?" Oscar asked, as he began to get up.

"I don't know," the police officer said.

Oscar headed for history class. He had missed most of English class. An inept young woman who told everyone to just read the textbook and be quiet was handling Mr. Meeker's classes.

Mr. Dunphy was usually smiling and joking as class began, but today he was quite somber. "We're all pretty upset this morning, you guys," he said. Mr. Dunphy called everybody "you guys." "Phil Meeker has been a teacher at Pico for almost ten years, and we all are feeling bad. So let's start class with a moment of silence. You folks who believe in prayer, say one for Mr. Meeker or send him good thoughts or vibes at this terrible time."

Oscar joined the ones who were praying. He really meant his prayer too. He didn't want Mr. Meeker to die. He was a human being, and nobody deserved to be beaten to death, plus Oscar worried they might blame him for the crime.

After class, a boy Oscar hardly knew fell in step beside him, speaking softly. "How about what happened to Meeker?" Derek Nichols said a little over a whisper.

"Yeah, bad business," Oscar said.

"You didn't like him, did you?" Derek asked.

"Huh? He was okay. Lot of kids didn't like him," Oscar said defensively.

"But he was really down on you, eh, Oscar? Everybody knew he was holding a grudge against you," Derek said.

Oscar looked at Derek. "That's stupid. He treated me just like he treated everybody else," he said.

"That's not what I hear," Derek said with a faint grin.

"So, what're you saying, man?" Oscar demanded.

"Nothing. I'm just saying nobody better mess with Oscar Quintero. No way," Derek said, a strange mixture of fear and admiration on his face. He hurried off before Oscar could say anything more.

Oscar felt like poor old Maitre Hauchecorne. He was surrounded by the faces of people he had known for years— all of them curious. Most were suspicious. Even when they said nothing, he could see the accusation in their eyes.

Oscar almost ran to his next class, math. He felt as if he were caught in some big machine that was spinning him around against his will and there was nothing he could do.

3 TWO DAYS AFTER he was attacked at Pico High School, Mr. Meeker remained in a coma. Danny's mother, Magda, met Oscar's mother at the supermarket on Saturday morning, and Oscar's mom came home very upset.

"Oscar," she said, even before she put down her heavy plastic bags, "what is this about you not getting along with Mr. Meeker this year? Magda Silva said it's all over the school that you hated the man!"

"They're just blowing smoke," Oscar said. "I'm not a hater. It's just that Mr. Meeker didn't like me, and he hassled me. He graded me down and stuff, but it wasn't any big thing."

"You never talked to me about this," his mom said. "If you were having problems with a teacher, why didn't you talk to me?"

"I'm telling you, Mom, it was no big deal. I just had the feeling that the guy didn't like me much, and I couldn't understand what his problem was. I talked to him—uh—a couple days ago and he said everything was cool," Oscar said.

"Magda was looking at me so funny in the store, Oscar, like she suspected something awful. I was frightened by the way she was looking at me. It was almost as if she thought you were the one who hurt Mr. Meeker," his mom said.

"Mom, you know that's stupid. That's the stupidest thing I've ever heard. She must have misunderstood something Danny said," Oscar said.

But inside, Oscar was feeling uneasy. It wasn't just Magda Silva having suspicious thoughts. Oscar could see the doubt in the eyes of many of the students at Pico. They were whispering behind Oscar's back, wondering . . . And now he could see questions in his mother's eyes.

Oscar's mom slowly unloaded her groceries. "Well, I am very upset by all this. I worry about you, Oscar. You are at a bad age. At your age, a boy needs a father, and you have none. Where is your father? Who knows? He is like the Santa Ana winds, blowing in and out and away. It's my fault. Such a stupid woman I am. Why did I marry such a man?" she said.

"Mom, don't get yourself crazy. Everything is okay," Oscar said. "Mr. Meeker got attacked by some criminal, that's all. There's nothing for you to worry about."

....

On Saturday afternoon, Oscar and Danny rode around in Danny's old pickup. "What'd you tell your mother about me and Mr. Meeker, Danny? She talked to my mom, and my mom threw a fit," Oscar said.

"I just told her Mr. Meeker was hassling you and you were mad about it. My mom blows everything up," Danny said.

Oscar continued, "I hope no kid from Pico did it. The law says kids who do big-time stuff like that get charged as adults."

"Maybe Meeker had some enemies we don't even know about," Danny said. "He's kind of a sneaky person. Nobody knows a lot about him. I asked Mr. Dunphy if the guy was married, and he said he thought he was divorced, but he wasn't sure. Imagine, and Dunphy is supposed to be a friend of Meeker's!"

"I know where Meeker lives," Oscar said. "When I had that job with the pizza place, I drove with the delivery guy. One day we delivered a pizza to Meeker. I ran in with it, and he tipped me 50 cents! Only 50 cents for a $12 pizza delivery."

"Oh, yeah? Show me how to get there," Danny said.

They drove around the block and onto the freeway. They got off at the second exit in a neighborhood of condos and apartments. The stucco buildings with their red tile roofs all looked alike, like the whole place was part of some big institution.

"Right there, the corner apartment. See the balcony with the hanging ivy?" Oscar said.

"Maybe we could stop, and you could ask the neighbors about the guy. Maybe they'd say something that'd tip us off to some enemies," Danny said.

"Are you crazy? The police are already suspicious of me. What would they think if people said I was nosing around where he lives?" Oscar groaned.

"Okay," Danny said. "I'll go see what I

can find out. You wait for me. I'll tell them I'm from the school newspaper, from the *Pico Press*, and I'm writing an article about our beloved teacher. After all, I do work as a gofer for the paper."

Danny returned shortly. "Hardly anybody knows the guy. He's like a spook. One dude said Meeker goes to the gym every morning at 5:00. Meeker is divorced. I found that out from an old lady who spends her life peering out the window. Oh, yeah, he's got a brother, and he came around sometimes. And there's a son. But nobody ever saw the son," Danny reported.

"Doesn't help, huh?" Oscar said. "Maybe it was just a random crime. Some creep looking for easy money . . ."

Danny shrugged. "The guy seems to lead a really dull life. The old lady who lives next door said he comes home every night at the same time, and he listens to public broadcasting. Or he plays classical music on the stereo. She said when the windows are open, you can hear everything. She said he never has visitors except for the brother. The lady said he was a very nice man because one day he carried her groceries for her," Danny said.

....

On Monday, the police returned to Pico High School. They didn't interview as many students as they had before, but they talked to Oscar again.

"You had a real problem with Mr. Meeker, didn't you, Oscar?" Sergeant Velez asked, his shrewd little eyes digging into Oscar. "We're getting that from a lot of different people. You were pretty ticked off about it."

"Nobody likes him," Oscar shot back. "You can ask around."

"You told me you talked to him earlier in the day that he was attacked. You told me you straightened things out, but that's not the story we're getting," Velez said.

Oscar glared at the police officer. "Look, I didn't have anything to do with what happened to Mr. Meeker. I didn't like the guy, okay? But I was home starting dinner for me and Mom when he got hit, okay?" Oscar said.

"Well, if we need to talk to you again,

we might ask you to come down to the station, Oscar," Velez said. He looked much more suspicious than he had before. Oscar figured that's how it worked in matters like this. After a few days, the police hone in on a likely suspect and start trying to build a case. But Oscar hadn't done anything!

When Oscar went to lunch in the school cafeteria, Tina joined him. Oscar and Tina hung out a lot, but they weren't dating or anything. They went to some beach parties and a couple of salsa concerts with other kids. But Oscar did like Tina more than he'd ever liked a girl before. He thought maybe something would come of their friendship.

"The police talked to you again, didn't they, Oscar?" Tina asked.

"Yeah. I guess a lot of people are ratting me out. Now the police are circling like I'm a dead wolf and they're vultures. And all the while the guy who really did it to Meeker is probably out there feeling no pain," Oscar said bitterly.

Tina didn't say anything. She quietly sipped her soda. Once or twice Oscar caught her staring at him. He thought the worst. Tina wasn't sure about him, either. Not even Tina. It had crossed her mind that maybe Oscar went over the edge and hit the guy.

Two boys came walking over to where Oscar and Tina sat. "Hey *muchacha*, don't say anything to get this guy mad," one of them said. "He's a bad dude."

"Yeah, you don't want to get on his bad side," the other boy laughed.

"That's so unfunny that it's pathetic," Tina said. "You guys go and blow bubbles or find a sandbox to play in."

Oscar was swept with new respect for Tina. She really stood up to those creeps.

"I get stuff like that all the time, Tina," he said. "It's like that poor guy in 'The Piece of String.' People want to believe the worst."

"Not all people," Tina said. "Just the kind of people who don't count much. Don't sweat it, Oscar. Nobody who knows you is going to think you savagely beat a 40-year-old English teacher."

Lindy Paul, another junior, was circulating a large get-well card for

Mr. Meeker. She worked her way over to where Oscar and Tina sat.

"Look at her," Tina said. "She thinks she's the hottest *chile* in the *enchilada*!"

"Hi, Tina," Lindy said. "Poor Mr. Meeker is still in a coma, and we're all just worried sick. I mean, I'm supposed to get everyone to write a little message for him in case he wakes up, you know, to give him courage. I don't know why they picked me to do it. I guess it's because they know I'll just run my feet off to get lots of signatures. Would you write something sweet, Tina?"

Tina scrawled a get-well wish and signed her name.

"I'm going to take the card to the hospital," Lindy said. "They won't let me into intensive care where he is, but his brother will probably take it. I'm riding down to the hospital with our counselor, Ms. Webb."

Lindy was already walking away when Oscar said, "I'll sign the card too, Lindy."

"Oh," Lindy said. "I didn't think . . . but that's great. I mean, I know you felt that Mr. Meeker didn't like you, but, you know, he just always felt bad because of that rumor you started about him. Remember? When we were all freshmen?"

Oscar had just started writing his message when Lindy mentioned the rumor. He almost dropped the pen. "What rumor? I don't know what you're talking about, Lindy."

"Oh, you remember," Lindy said. "I'm sure you didn't mean any harm, but it was at a beach party at Karla's house. You said your father went to college with Mr. Meeker at CSUN and that Mr. Meeker cheated on his master's exams and almost got kicked out of school . . ."

"Are you crazy?" Oscar almost screamed. "I never went to any beach party at Karla's house, and my father dropped out of high school. He never even *saw* Cal State University at Northridge. I never said anything like that about Mr. Meeker!"

Lindy looked surprised. "But I was sure it was you . . . I was always sure it was you. I remember asking Mr. Meeker if the rumor was true, and he got really upset. He said he never cheated on an exam in his life," she said. She was rapidly turning pale. Her eyes widened, and she realized she had made a serious mistake.

4 "YOU *TOLD* MEEKER that I said he cheated on his master's exams, didn't you?" Oscar demanded.

"No, no," Lindy stammered, looking frightened. "I didn't. I mean I didn't say anything recently. It was like almost two years ago, and he started talking about his master's exams . . . and one thing led to another."

"And being the gossip you are, you just couldn't resist telling him about the nasty guy who was spreading a dirty rumor about him. That was one way to earn brownie points with Mr. Meeker. Good little Lindy Paul wants to warn the teacher that bad Oscar Quintero is ruining his reputation with lies . . . I'm sure you got all wide-eyed and assured Meeker that you didn't believe a word of the rumor." Tina's voice dripped with disgust. "Honestly, Lindy, you have caused more trouble around here with your gossiping! It's like deadly poison you have dripping from your saliva!"

"I didn't mean any harm," Lindy said. "I mean, I really believed Oscar had said it, and I didn't remember him saying not to tell anybody. I remember you standing there by the pool and telling us all Mr. Meeker was a cheat!"

"I bet you got Oscar mixed up with Roddy Sanchez," Tina said. "Remember, we all hung out with Roddy that first year. He played football, and he was a big guy like Oscar. Then he went to another school in his sophomore year. His father was a chemist, and he had gone to CSUN. Yeah, it had to be Roddy. He was a gossip too. Guys can be as rotten as girls like that."

"You mixed me up with Roddy and got Mr. Meeker to hate me all this time?" Oscar asked furiously. "All this time Meeker has been hassling me because of some stupid gossip you spread? Thanks a lot, Lindy!"

"I'm sorry," Lindy said tearfully. "I really did think you'd said it, Oscar. I'm sorry."

"Give me a break," Tina snapped. "Don't go all weepy on us now. You know better than to gossip. When we were sophomores, you spread a horrible rumor about Isabel

Ybarra, and she got so depressed she dropped out."

"*Everybody* was saying she was trashy, not just me," Lindy argued. "You *know* the way she dressed and what the boys called her."

"Yeah, and you carried every dirty little story back to her, very sweetly, of course. Like you were trying to help her, assuring her all the time that you didn't believe a word of what kids were saying . . . but what you did was convince her that everybody thought she was garbage that belonged at the curb on pickup day!" Tina said.

Lindy grabbed the get-well card and fled.

Oscar buried his face in his hands and shook his head in disbelief. "Oh, man, look what she did to me! Meeker never would have treated me like that if she hadn't told him I was spreading lies about him. Now everybody knows how much I hated the guy, and if he dies, they'll probably nail me with a murder charge. I'll probably end up on death row!" he said.

"Oscar, come on, don't freak on me," Tina said.

Oscar looked at the girl. "Do you realize how many innocent guys have been convicted of murder and put on death row? Then later when they used DNA, they pulled a whole bunch of guys off death row. So what does that tell you? I already have a motive. I hated the guy and everybody knows it. I don't have an alibi. Maybe some fibers from my jacket are on his coat. Who knows how that happens? I was at his desk . . . anything could be there," he said.

"Oscar, don't go crazy," Tina said. "Some criminal attacked Meeker, and they'll catch the guilty guy soon."

"All those poor dudes on death row. I'm sure they hoped the real criminals would get caught before the electric charge went through them. But it didn't happen for some of them," Oscar groaned. "If only I'd known that Lindy was feeding that lie to Meeker. I could have straightened it out long ago, and none of this would be happening."

"Gossip is so evil," Tina said. "My grandmother always told me that when you spread gossip, it's like taking a pillow to the top of a windy hill, and cutting it open, and letting all the feathers fly. You can't ever take it back any more than you could recapture all the feathers."

Oscar tried to pay attention to his afternoon classes, but it was a struggle. He kept imagining Sergeant Velez coming to the school or the apartment and placing Oscar under arrest, handcuffing him, and putting him in the patrol car.

Oscar's favorite class was biology, and his favorite teacher was Ms. Lisa Windermere. She was a beautiful and brilliant young woman who made science come alive for all of her students. Largely because of her, Oscar had begun to consider a career in science for himself. Ms. Windermere even got the poorest students interested in science with her unbounded enthusiasm. Now Oscar walked into biology, determined not to let the cloud over his head ruin the class completely.

Ms. Windermere always carried her briefcase bulging with corrected tests and material for class when she came in. She always seemed actually happy to tackle her period 5 class, which came near the end of the day when many teachers were already dragging. But this afternoon, she seemed to be limping, and the right side of her face was obviously heavily made-up to conceal some injuries. A horrible thought occurred to Oscar. Had Ms. Windermere been attacked too? Was there some madman loose on the campus targeting teachers?

"Look at her," Oscar whispered to Danny. "She looks awful."

"Yeah, all beat up," Danny agreed.

Lindy Paul raised her hand immediately. "Ms. Windermere, what happened to you? You weren't attacked like poor Mr. Meeker were you?" she asked.

Ms. Windermere shook her head. "No, nothing like that. I'm actually fine, though I look a little worse for wear. We were hiking in the foothills, and I took a nasty tumble. I went flying down into a rocky ravine. I guess I'm lucky I didn't break anything. I'm afraid I got bruised up pretty good, but it's mostly cosmetic." She tried to smile to reassure her students, but moving her facial muscles made her wince with pain.

Ms. Windermere started her lecture then, apparently anxious to end the conversation about her injuries. Oscar figured she was probably embarrassed.

Soon Oscar heard whispers behind him in class.

"I bet her husband hit her," Susie Anders said.

"Do you think so?" Lindy asked with a quiver of excitement in her voice. There was nothing that charmed Lindy as much as the scent of a scandal, something that produced juicy gossip. She enjoyed speculating about it, then sowing it like seeds in a freshly ploughed furrow.

"I saw her husband once," another girl joined in and added to the story. "He looks mean, like he's capable of anything."

"Girls," Ms. Windermere said, catching the buzz of conversation but not hearing its content. "We're talking about genetics now, and it's a really important unit. If you continue talking among yourselves, I'm afraid you'll miss all this good stuff about internal substances and processes that make us who and what we are."

As Oscar was leaving Pico High that day with Danny, he overheard several students discussing Ms. Windermere.

"Lindy Paul is like a virus," Oscar said. "She spreads rumors and suspicions, and pretty soon it's all over the school."

"Yeah," Danny said. "She needs just a shred of a story, and she's off and running."

"Hey, Quintero," came a vaguely familiar voice. Oscar turned to see Lee Gavon, a former student at Pico. He had dropped out in his sophomore year like many kids did. Like Oscar, he was big and athletic. But unlike Oscar, Lee had not kept his grades up and could not play with the Pico Panthers.

"How's it going, Lee?" Oscar asked. "Haven't seen you in a long time."

"Yeah, I've been in Texas working in construction with my uncle. I miss you guys. I feel like I'm going nowhere. Remember when we used to talk about football scholarships and hitting the NFL?" Lee said in a forlorn voice.

"Yeah, man," Oscar said.

"I heard what happened to Meeker," Lee said, a big grin coming to his face. "It couldn't have happened to a better target. It was Meeker who messed up my GPA so much I had to drop all athletic stuff, you know."

"I didn't know that," Oscar said.

"Yeah. I wasn't doing all that great in my other classes, but I was hanging on to a C. But when Meeker hit me with that F in English, my GPA went right down the tubes, and that's when I dropped school. I begged the guy not to flunk me, but he went deaf on me, you know?" Lee said bitterly.

Oscar looked at the other boy and wondered. Could it have been Lee Gavon in that twilit parking lot when Mr. Meeker was walking to his car?

"I'm sorry things didn't work out for you, Lee. But maybe you could come back to school, huh?" Oscar said.

Lee laughed bitterly. "Yeah, right. I'm like a year behind everybody else, and look at the size of me. I'm almost 18 now, man. Wouldn't it be a joke to see me sitting in class with a bunch of 16-year-olds?

Lee Gavon, the dummy," he said.

"What about adult school or something?" Oscar asked.

"Yeah, I could, I guess. But I miss the scene, man. You hear what I'm saying? I miss the football, the friends, hanging out. He took all that away from me, Meeker did. I'm glad somebody bashed his head in. He had it coming. There's a lot of ways to kill somebody. It's not just by stopping them from breathing, man. You can kill somebody's spirit, their soul. That's what Meeker did," Lee said.

Oscar shook his head. "Don't be like that, Lee. Hate is like acid eating you. Nobody deserves to get what Meeker got, and nobody has the right to deliver that kind of retribution anyway. I know what I'm talking about, man. I felt like you. He was hassling me too, and the hatred was getting to me, *hermano*," Oscar said.

A half-smile lingered on Lee's face. "You aren't the one who whacked him, are you? There's some talk that you did. I was shooting pool, and some guys were talking like that. I wouldn't hold it against you, Oscar. Somebody had to take him out," Lee said.

"I didn't do it," Oscar snapped. "I wouldn't do something like that. Never!"

"Okay, okay, don't spit fire, man," Lee said. "I don't care who did it. I'm just glad it happened. Well, see you around." He turned and headed away.

"You think he did it?" Danny asked Oscar when Lee was gone.

Oscar shrugged. "I don't know. I'm not going to be like Lindy Paul and say he did," he said.

But Lee Gavon was strong and mean enough for the job. And he was sure glad about it.

5 WHEN OSCAR GOT HOME, he heard a man's voice in the kitchen. The only voices he usually heard in their apartment were the voices of his sisters and their children.

"*Hijo*," his dad shouted when Oscar appeared. His father was heavier than Oscar remembered. He came over and gave Oscar a bear hug, and his big stomach rammed into Oscar's body. Oscar had not seen his father since last Christmas. He hadn't expected to see him until Christmas came around again. That was the drill. Christmas always and sometimes birthdays.

"Hi, Papa," Oscar said.

The man's black hair was flecked with gray. He looked much older than his 40 years. His stomach hung over his belt like a kangaroo's pouch. Oscar made a mental note to never get that way, to work out all his life and always stay fit.

"How are you, *hijo*? You taking care of

business, eh?" his dad asked.

"You've been away too long, Papa," Oscar said. "I hoped you'd come for my birthday in April."

"I planned to. I was on the way. I left the oil rig in Louisiana that I was working on, and I got sick going through Texas. I couldn't make it home," his dad said.

Oscar knew it was all a lie. His dad's lies were numerous and shallow. They slipped from his lips like water over rocks, smoothly. He probably didn't even know anymore that he was lying. His lies became fact with repeated telling.

Oscar's mom was at the kitchen sink, her back to the conversation. She was washing dishes vigorously. Oscar's mom did not hate his dad. She wasn't the type who could hate anyone. But she was tired of him, and she had no more patience with him.

"So what's this I hear about some crazy people trying to blame you for busting up some teacher, Oscar?" his dad asked.

Now Oscar understood why his father was here. He would not have come around until Christmas, but his mom had called him. She was that upset, that worried. Oscar's dad was not a good parent, but he was still a parent, and his mom must have reminded him of that. She rarely got in touch with her ex-husband, but she always knew where to get him if necessary. He was at least responsible enough to keep in touch by furnishing a current address. Last year, when Oscar's oldest sister had had a difficult pregnancy and serious bleeding, his dad had appeared and stayed at the hospital for two days.

"That's all nonsense, Pa," Oscar said. "I had a problem with the guy because some creep at school told him I was spreading lies about him. I was on his bad list because of this gossip. But all that had nothing to do with him getting hurt. I had nothing to do with that."

Oscar's dad grabbed Oscar around the neck, giving him a squeeze. "Yeah, yeah. I know you wouldn't get mixed up in something like that. You're too good a kid. So doesn't your teacher know who hit him?" his dad asked.

From the sink, Oscar's mom said, "I

told you, Fred. The man is in a coma. He may never wake up. I know. I work at the hospital. I may be just a humble CNA, but I know what's going on. I've got a lot of friends who are RNs, and they tell me it looks very bad for that man. Even if he does live, he will probably be impaired. He may have no memory of what happened."

"I think a doper hit him, Dad," Oscar said. "Some guy wanting drug money. There's a lot of that around here."

"Yes," his mom said from the sink. "We live in a bad neighborhood. It's too bad. Both my sisters who got married after I did have long since moved away from here. Now they live in nice suburbs where there's not so much crime. But what can I do?" His mom was reminding his dad, as she often did, how much he had failed his family. He not only left them, but he did not provide for them.

Oscar's dad ignored the comment. He returned his attention to Oscar. "Do you want to go for a taco, *hijo*?"

His mom turned from the sink, her face hard. "You have your homework, Oscar.

Don't forget your homework."

His mom resented the way her ex-husband returned so infrequently and then played the part of the fun dad who took his children out and spent money on them. He did the same with his daughters. He would bring some ridiculously expensive gift for them or their children, hoping that all would be forgiven. And it often was. His mom did not want him forgiven by anybody, especially his children.

"It's okay, Mom. I don't have any homework tonight. I did it all at school," Oscar said. He was eager for a little time with his father, time alone with him, away from his mom's bitterness.

Sure, Oscar thought, his mom had a right to be bitter. He understood that. His dad had done a terrible thing leaving his family like that, sending only sporadic support that they couldn't depend upon. But Freddy Quintero was still Oscar's father, the only father he would ever have. Oscar did not know why his parents' marriage went so wrong. He guessed it was mostly his dad's fault, but his mom wasn't the easiest person in the world to live with, either. She could nag, and she held grudges. It was hard for her to forgive anything, even a small thing.

"Okay, go on," his mom said. "But don't be late coming back. I've got enough to worry about."

Oscar and his father walked down to the taco shop on the corner. It had been in business for 30 years, passed from father to sons. Everybody knew the Narvaez family, Papa Juan and sons Jimmy and Benedicto.

As they walked, Oscar's father said, "I don't blame your mother for how she feels. I was a bad husband and a worse father. But, Oscar, we, your mother and I, we made a big mistake. We were only a couple years older than you are now when we got married. And then your sister, Carmen, was on the way. A baby coming to a couple of kids who hadn't grown up yet themselves and knew nothing about life."

"Yeah," Oscar said. At least that was something both his parents agreed on. They had married too young.

"Here I was, a teenaged guy, and I had a wife and a kid and a job at the car wash! I couldn't handle it. I just hung out with my friends like I had before I was married. I felt comfortable there. Your mother kept running home to *abuela*, her mother. What else could she do? We tried to get it together, but we never could. We were too stupid, Oscar. Your sisters made the same mistakes. That's what makes you so special, *hijo*. You're not going to ditch high school and get some chump-change job. You're going to go to college and make something out of your life. That's why the stupid thing with the teacher has to be cleared up. A thing like this can't be allowed to mess you up," his dad said.

"I know, Dad. But what can I do?" Oscar groaned.

They went into the taco stand, and Oscar's dad greeted Jimmy Narvaez. "Jimmy and I were homies in the old days," his dad explained, as he embraced his friend.

"We had some good times, *hermano*," Jimmy said.

"Jimmy, you hear anything on the street

about who took that teacher down?" Oscar's dad asked.

"No," Jimmy said. "Usually when a gang member does something, everybody knows. Nobody talks, but everybody knows. Now there's nothing. Absolutely nothing. Everybody is really surprised that something like this happened right at the school."

"You know, Jimmy, my boy here did not get along with Mr. Meeker, the teacher. Some fools are trying to blame him," Oscar's dad said scornfully.

"Get outta here," Jimmy said. "Not Oscar. I've known Oscar since he was a tiny *niño*!"

"Yeah, but the police have talked to him twice," Oscar's dad said. "I was thinking, maybe Mr. Meeker led a double life or something. Maybe he got hit for something we don't even know about."

"He's such a dull little guy, though," Oscar said. "I can't imagine Meeker getting mixed up with criminals of any kind. His neighbor at the condo said all he did was listen to symphony music and stuff."

Oscar and his father took their tacos to a booth and sat down.

"They make the best tacos in the world right here," his dad said, biting into the soft tortilla. "I don't know what they put in the salsa, but it's fabulous!"

"Yeah," Oscar agreed. He thought about Lee Gavon and how he blamed Mr. Meeker for ruining his life—how happy he was that Mr. Meeker had been attacked. Oscar wondered if he should mention that to his father. Maybe that was an angle his dad would want to look into. But then Oscar decided not to say anything about Lee. Lee was a loner, probably just shooting off his mouth. He probably had nothing to do with the attack. Oscar didn't want to be like Lindy Paul, pointing the finger of suspicion at people who might be innocent.

"So, Oscar, how do you get along in school with your other teachers?" his dad asked.

"Great. My teachers really like me. I've never gotten a bad mark from anybody. I'm getting mostly A's. I'm getting an A in biology. I have this lady teacher,

Ms. Windermere, and she's super. I love that class. It's made me think maybe I'll go for a career in science," Oscar said.

"Well, they can't stick you with something you didn't do, Oscar," his dad said firmly. "You just ignore the creeps at school who're making it rough on you. You're a good kid, Oscar. You're going to make your mother and me really proud."

Oscar's dad explained later that night that he wished he could stick around to see if there was anything else he could do, but if he didn't go back to his job in Louisiana, he'd be unemployed. He slipped a hundred dollar bill into Oscar's mom's purse, winked at Oscar, and left.

After his dad was gone, Oscar told his mother about the one hundred dollar bill. She spat. "That's just like him," his mom said. "The big gesture. He thinks it makes it all okay, but it doesn't. We need him now, and he's gone."

"It'll be okay, Mom," Oscar said. "I didn't do anything. Somebody else hurt Mr. Meeker, and they'll find who did it."

"Pray he wakes up and remembers who hurt him, Oscar," his mom said. "I'm stopping at the church and lighting a candle after work tomorrow. I'm doing it for the teacher so he wakes up and can tell the truth."

Oscar's mom left for work at 10:00. She went on duty at 10:30 and finished in the morning. When she got home, Oscar would be eating his breakfast and getting ready for school.

After his mother left, Oscar felt restless. He didn't feel like going to bed just yet. He needed somebody to hang out with. He wanted to be with people and to talk. And there was nobody home to tell him it was stupid to go out in the street at this hour.

It was cool and the night sky was peppered with stars. Oscar had never paid much attention to the stars until he met Ms. Windermere. She introduced her students to all aspects of science, and now Oscar looked at the whole world in a new way. He got all interested in stars, constellations, and planets. Now, whenever he went out at night, he would glance skyward and check out the sky, maybe even recognize the phase the moon was in.

When Oscar got to the corner, there were some homeboys standing around. Oscar spotted Ivan and Al, two gang members who had dropped out of Pico during their sophomore year. They weren't hard-core, and they had joined the gang because there wasn't much warmth at home. The gang was the closest thing to a family they had.

"Hey, Oscar Quintero," Ivan called out. "You are bad, man!"

The way Ivan said it, it was a compliment.

"You come to hang with us, Oscar?" Al asked.

Oscar stared at the boys. They had been just like him a couple of years ago. They were part of the group that went skateboarding and played one-on-one basketball until it was too dark to see the net.

"No stress, man," Ivan said. "We don't care what you've done, you hear?"

6 SUDDENLY OSCAR FELT SO SICK of being blamed for something he hadn't done that he stopped caring, at least temporarily. Like the old saying went, if you've got the name you may as well play the game. His mother wouldn't be home until morning, and there was no sleep in him. So why not hang out with Ivan and Al?

The three boys climbed into a banged-up old Mazda and Ivan asked Oscar, "What's happening at Pico High since we left? It still as lame as it used to be?"

"It's okay, I guess," Oscar said.

"When I went there, all the lady teachers were ugly," Ivan said. "But the other day, I drove past the school, and here was this amazing chick getting into a car in the faculty parking lot. Who's she?"

"Probably Ms. Windermere," Oscar said. "She's pretty cool. She teaches biology. She's smart and nice."

"She married?" Ivan asked. "She looks like a senior."

"Yeah, she's married," Oscar said, "but she's young. She's like 25 or something, younger than one of my sisters."

"What went down the other night, dude?" Al asked. "You and the old man get in a fight or what?"

"Yeah," Ivan joined in, "did it get out of hand, man?"

"I didn't have anything to do with that," Oscar said. "I was home cutting up iceberg lettuce when that happened."

Ivan laughed. "You are one cool dude, man. Don't share with nobody. That's the way," he said.

"It's the truth. I never touched that man," Oscar said, growing angry. "It's not my style to beat up some skinny 40-year-old man like that."

"Yeah, Meeker is an old man now," Ivan said. "I remember he taught my brother like about five years ago. He flunked Roberto. I remember that. Course, Roberto never studied or anything. I remember when my brother was in Meeker's class, Meeker was getting divorced from his old lady. Meeker had a kid, about 15. He didn't go to school at

Pico. He went to a nice magnet school across town. But he'd come to Pico sometimes and fight with the old man. A real whacked-out kid. Meeker tried to shush the little punk."

"I wonder where his son is now?" Oscar asked.

"Who knows? Probably on the streets. He was stoned all the time. I think Meeker was afraid of him. One time Meeker called the police on him. They took the kid away. The kid was smashing the windows in Meeker's car," Ivan said, chuckling at the memory.

Oscar was intrigued by the new information. He drove around with Ivan and Al for another hour, then they stopped for pizza. They dropped Oscar home at 2:00 in the morning. Oscar couldn't get Mr. Meeker's son off his mind. Maybe the son was the person who came to the faculty parking lot and attacked his father. Maybe he harbored a grudge against his father over the divorce. Oscar had heard that murder victims are most often related to, or friends with, their attackers. And Mr. Meeker was beaten so savagely that it seemed it was an act of passion, or hatred, rather than a random crime.

....

The next day after school, Oscar went to the Community Hospital. He didn't expect to see Mr. Meeker, but he hoped he might get to talk to Mr. Meeker's brother and perhaps learn what had happened to the son. Oscar stopped at a gift shop before arriving at the hospital. He bought an apple-shaped ceramic coffee cup. The message on the cup said, Get well, Teacher.

Oscar carried his gift in a paper bag into the lobby of the hospital. He asked at the desk where Mr. Meeker was, and a silver-haired volunteer told him that the patient was in intensive care and only close family members could see him. But then she added, "His brother came in about an hour ago. He often drinks coffee in the lounge near ICU. You could give him the gift for Mr. Meeker."

Oscar rode the elevator to the third floor. He walked down the hall, steering around nurses pushing patients in wheelchairs with IVs attached to them. Oscar found just two people in the visitors' lounge—an elderly lady and a man who looked like Mr. Meeker, only a bit older.

Before Oscar had the chance to talk to the man, Ms. Windermere arrived with a beautiful floral display for Mr. Meeker. "Oh, hi, Oscar, did you bring something for Mr. Meeker too?"

"Yeah, just a little something," Oscar said.

Ms. Windermere seemed to know Mr. Meeker's brother. She had probably been here before and met him. "Dave," she said, "this is Oscar Quintero, one of your brother's students from Pico."

"Hi," Oscar said to the man.

"Hello. Thanks for coming, both of you. This has all been so terrible," the man said.

Oscar knew it was now or never to find out about Mr. Meeker's son. So he said, "Uh . . . I feel sorry for Mr. Meeker's son. He's like a kid, I guess. Uh, tell him we're all pulling for Mr. Meeker at Pico High School."

Philip Meeker's brother got a strange look on his face. "Yes, thanks," he said. "I am going to be with him, with my brother now. He doesn't know I'm there but . . . " He gathered up the floral display and Oscar's cup and hurried down the hall to ICU.

"Shall we get some coffee at the machine, Oscar?" Ms. Windermere asked.

"Sure," Oscar said.

They sat in the lounge, drinking their coffee. She was so beautiful that it gave Oscar goose bumps just to be sitting this close to her. Even with the bruises on her face, she was lovely. And she treated Oscar like no other teacher did, like a friend.

"It was so thoughtful of you to bring that gift, Oscar. I brought a card the teachers signed and the flowers from the staff. Poor Mr. Meeker. All these gifts, and he can't even appreciate them. Hopefully he'll wake up soon and know how much we care about him," she said.

"You know, Ms. Windermere," Oscar began. He was emboldened enough by her warmth to bare his feelings. "I feel really bad about all this because Mr. Meeker and I had problems. It makes me feel terrible that this happened after we argued. See, a long time ago, somebody told Mr. Meeker that I'd lied about him, but it never happened. That turned Mr. Meeker against me, and I got mad that he seemed to hate me for no reason. It wasn't until after he got attacked that I learned why he seemed to hate me."

"Oh, Oscar, that's a shame. But none of it was your fault. I'm sure he'll come out of the coma very soon, and then he'll understand about everything," Ms. Windermere said.

"I wish, you know, the police would find the guy who attacked him," Oscar said. "If he wakes up, he can probably identify the guy."

"He was struck from behind, Oscar. That's what his brother told me. It appears that someone was hiding behind the shrubbery, those oleander bushes. And when Mr. Meeker walked up, he never saw what hit him," Ms. Windermere said.

Oscar noticed that the teacher's hands were trembling as she spoke. He was startled to see that. She seemed so calm and self-assured. Why would her hands be trembling like that? Oscar quickly looked away. He didn't want to embarrass her.

As they walked out of the hospital together, Ms. Windermere asked. "Oscar, how did you know Mr. Meeker had a son? We talked quite often, and he never told me that."

"I don't know. Somebody told me, I guess. This guy, he said Mr. Meeker didn't get along with his son. Maybe the boy doesn't even know what happened to his father," Oscar said.

"That would be too bad," Ms. Windermere said. "We like to think families are like those people on those old TV comedies, but it's not so. A lot of families are . . . troubled."

"Yeah," Oscar said, trying not to notice that her hands still trembled.

"How will you get home, Oscar?" she asked.

"I came by bus," Oscar said.

"I'll drive you home," Ms. Windermere offered. "No need for you to wait for the bus."

"You don't have to do that," Oscar said.

"But I want to," she said, smiling. "I like you very much, Oscar. I expect great things from you. When I'm old and gray, I believe I'll see you accepting some prestigious prize for a research breakthrough."

It was the nicest compliment Oscar could ever remember getting. He would remember it for the rest of his life. He would try to live up to it too. "Thanks, Ms. Windermere," Oscar said appreciatively.

Oscar thought Ms. Windermere was the nicest teacher he had ever met. Never mind that she was so beautiful. She had curly auburn hair and incredible green eyes. Oscar thought she was prettier than any woman he had ever seen. It was amazing to him that she was also so intelligent and so charming and interesting. She already had her master's degree in biology, and she was working on her doctorate. Last year she won a much-coveted award for innovative teaching methods in science.

As they drove the short distance between the hospital and Oscar's home,

Ms. Windermere said, "You know, Mr. Meeker is a very strict and even harsh teacher, but he does care about his students. He surely isn't the most popular teacher at Pico High School, but he wants his students to succeed in life. He believes he is accomplishing his goal by being tough. He has a very caring side too, which students don't often see."

Oscar wasn't so sure about that. He never saw much tenderness in Mr. Meeker's sharp, sarcastic remarks, but then maybe that was his way of bringing out the best in his students.

"Actually," Ms. Windermere said, "when I had some personal problems a while ago, it was Mr. Meeker's compassion and concern that got me through a very rough spot. I owe him a debt of gratitude for that. When you're hurting, it's not easy to find someone who will be there for you, and he was. It's just so tragic that something so terrible has happened to him. It's heartbreaking. Of course, every person is valuable, but you expect ugly things like this to happen to people who're involved with a bad crowd, drug dealers and the like. But I guess it's foolish to think like that. Awful things do happen to good people."

"Yeah," Oscar said.

Oscar thanked the teacher for the ride, got out, and hurried toward his apartment. Ms. Windermere seemed to care a lot for Mr. Meeker. That must have been the reason for her to tremble like that. Obviously, Oscar thought, the guy did have a side that he, Oscar, never saw.

Of course Ms. Windermere was such a kind, caring person that maybe she threw her heart into everyone's problems. That was one of the qualities that made her such a beautiful person. Like last year when a Vietnamese girl joined the class, Ms. Windermere went out of her way to tutor the girl, who was having a language problem. The girl was very bright, and Ms. Windermere wanted to make sure she didn't fall behind because of the language barrier. Due to the teacher's hard work, the girl was now excelling in class.

Oscar thought that if he were about eight years older or Ms. Windermere were eight years younger, he could easily fall in love with her. Maybe, Oscar allowed, he was even now a little bit in love with her.

7 OSCAR, TINA, DANNY, and Danny's friend Yvette went to the beach Friday night to roast hot dogs in a fire ring. They arrived around 9:00.

"Ms. Windermere wants us to go to the wetlands next month for a field trip," Yvette said. "That sounds so fun."

"I like field trips anyway," Danny said. "Gets us out of school."

"Hey," Tina said, "Did you guys know that Ms. Windermere has a niece who's a freshman at Pico?"

"No," Oscar said. "Who is she?"

"Sandy Bailey," Tina said. "She's really cute. When they had cheerleader tryouts, she was competing. Everybody really liked her."

"Sandy Bailey?" Danny repeated. "Yeah, I know her. I saw the tryouts. She's something else."

Yvette nudged Danny in mock jealousy. "You're always looking at pretty girls," she said. "It's a wonder your eyeballs don't pop out of your head!"

"Ms. Windermere is pretty too," Oscar said. "She's the prettiest teacher I ever saw."

Danny laughed. "You in love with our biology teacher, dude?"

"No, she's too old for me," Oscar admitted. "But if she wasn't . . ."

The moonlight splashed silver on the ocean waves. Oscar stared out across what seemed like an endless dark panorama of heaving water. He was trying to enjoy the night, but he kept thinking about Mr. Meeker and what was going to happen to him. If he died, what would happen to Oscar? In a murder case, the police would be even more eager to find the attacker.

Oscar wondered if the case would just hang out there for a long time. It would be like "The Piece of String." The police never arrested Hauchecorne, but everybody in the town of Goderville always believed he was guilty. Is that how it would be for Oscar? Would a cloud of suspicion hang forever over this head? Years from now when there were class reunions, would the subject come up?

Would there be whispers? Do you think Oscar Quintero was the one who killed Mr. Meeker? Do you really think it was him? It would be a dark stain on Oscar's reputation that would never fully go away unless the real attacker was caught.

Yvette was wiping mustard off her chin as she finished her hot dog. Then Danny squirted some mustard in Oscar's direction as a gag.

"Hey," Oscar said, "knock it off, man." Some of the mustard hit Oscar's T-shirt, and he was having trouble wiping it off. Danny aimed the mustard squirter again, and Yvette reached up and grabbed the bottle away from him.

"Can't you see Oscar's mad?" she asked.

Oscar saw something close to fear in Yvette's eyes, almost as if she dreaded rousing Oscar's ire.

"Yvette, I'm not going to explode or anything," Oscar said. "I'm used to Danny acting like a five-year-old!"

"I know," Yvette said, smiling slightly, "but everybody knows you've got a short fuse, Oscar . . . I mean, I don't want you guys fighting or anything."

"You act like Oscar is Godzilla or something," Tina said crossly. She caught it too, Yvette's strange, fearful look.

Oscar stared at Yvette and said, "You heard all the rumors about me and Mr. Meeker, didn't you? You're not so sure I wasn't the guy who smashed his head, are you?"

"No," Yvette said quickly. "That's not true. I mean, what do I know?"

"You think I beat up Mr. Meeker, and now I'll get so mad at Danny that maybe I'll bust his head too. Right?" Oscar asked bitterly. Anger and frustration flooded Oscar's soul. The tide of suspicion was rolling over him, and there wasn't anything he could do about it.

"I didn't mean anything," Yvette said anxiously. "Why are you getting so mad? I just didn't want Danny squirting mustard at people. I don't want any trouble. My mom doesn't even know I'm here at the beach with guys. She thinks I'm at a girlfriend's house, and I don't want anything bad to happen."

Oscar wanted to leave, but the four of them had come in Danny's truck. Oscar didn't want to sit on the sand anymore roasting hot dogs with Yvette looking at him like he was a ticking time bomb.

"Let's take a walk down the beach, Tina," Oscar said suddenly.

"Sure," Tina said, as if she understood exactly where Oscar was coming from.

When Oscar and Tina had walked a ways, she grasped Oscar's hand. "I know Yvette hurt you by acting that way, but it was just out of stupidity. She didn't mean any harm."

"Yeah, but it gives you a good idea how a lot of kids feel about me, Tina. They think I hurt Meeker. They think I'm some kind of madman. Look, there goes that big, brutal hulk, Oscar Quintero. Don't mess with him if you like breathing in and out. Tina, it's driving me crazy. I wake up in the morning thinking about it, and I go to bed at night thinking about it. I'm afraid it won't ever end," Oscar said.

"The police will solve it," Tina said in a halfhearted voice.

"Mr. Meeker didn't even see who hit him," Oscar said. "Ms. Windermere told me he was struck from behind. I guess his brother told her that because his head is, you know, bashed in from the back. There's no reason to be sure the police will get the right guy. Crimes like this are sometimes never solved."

"Oscar, you've got to be positive," Tina said. "You're running yourself into the ground with all this negative stuff."

Oscar stopped and turned toward Tina, taking her small, brown hands in his big hands. "Tell me the truth, Tina. Haven't you ever thought, if only for a minute, that maybe I *was* the one who hurt Mr. Meeker? That I hated the guy so much that I just lost it that night?"

"No," Tina said. "Not for one minute, not for a millisecond have I ever thought you did it, and I resent that you even asked me such a question. You would never hurt anybody. Anybody who really knows you knows that."

Oscar smiled at Tina. "Thanks," he said.

They walked on down the beach, kicking rubbery kelp aside and pausing to watch a sailboat making its way through the night, white sails against the blackness. "Sometimes I wish I could go to sea like young guys did a long time ago," Oscar said. "Just run off to sea and put this whole thing behind me."

....

On Monday morning Oscar sat in English listening to the substitute teacher, a gray-haired man named Weber, talking about short stories. Mr. Weber was not a very good teacher. He was retired, and he just took substitute work to supplement his retirement income. He was just going through the motions. There were rumors that the position would soon be filled by a long-term sub. Nobody really expected that Mr. Meeker would be back anytime soon, if at all.

Oscar's mind wandered as he sat in the dull English class. He wondered about Mr. Meeker's son. He'd be about 20 now. Oscar wondered if he knew his father was lying critically injured in the hospital. Oscar recalled what Ivan had told him, how the boy seemed to hate his father. How the father once called the police because he feared his son.

Maybe Mr. Meeker's own son had

attacked him. Maybe the guy was on the street now, using drugs. Maybe he was stoned out of his mind, nursing old grudges against his father.

Oscar wondered if there was any way he could find Mr. Meeker's son and talk to him. It was a long shot, but Oscar couldn't just sit and wait for the dark clouds to thicken over his head.

After school, Danny drove Oscar to the arcade where Ivan and his friends hung out. Both boys went in, and they immediately spotted Ivan.

"Hey, dude," Ivan said, grinning. "You beginning to enjoy this scene?"

"I'd like to find Mr. Meeker's son and talk to him," Oscar said. "You got any idea where he is?"

"I don't know. Maybe my brother would know. You can find him down at the pool hall. I think the Meeker kid comes in there sometimes," Ivan said.

Danny and Oscar drove down to the pool hall and looked around for Ivan's brother, Rob. Soon they spotted a boy who looked just like Ivan, only older and a little heavier. He had bloodshot eyes and he moved in a restless way.

"Your brother, Ivan, said we might find Meeker here," Oscar said.

"Brian Meeker?" Rob asked. He grinned, showing his missing front tooth. "Police have been here already. They talked to the guy. Me and Brian hung out when I went to Pico. He went to some private school, but we got together a lot. What do you want to see him for?"

"I'd just like to talk to him about stuff. I'm a student from Mr. Meeker's English class. You know about what happened to Mr. Meeker, don't you?" Oscar said.

Rob nodded. "Got his head busted." He looked Oscar up and down. "You a dopehead, man? You don't look like one. You have nice clear eyes, and you don't smell like a dopehead. You look like one of those straight-arrow dudes who do their homework every night and never hang with gang members," he said.

"I don't mess with drugs," Oscar said. "Do you think you could tell me where to find Brian Meeker?"

"Why not?" came a voice from the darkest corner of the pool hall. A sallow-faced young man who bore a great resemblance to Philip Meeker stepped out of the dark. He held a pool cue in one hand as he danced into view, slashing the air between himself and Oscar with the shaft.

"That's how I did it," he cried. "I got the old man with this. I whacked him and he went down! Bye, bye, Daddy!" He laughed maniacally and kept slashing the air with the cue.

8 "YOU'RE BRIAN MEEKER?" Oscar asked the young man, though he had no doubt. The physical resemblance was just too strong.

"None other," Brian said. "Who would have believed it? Private schools all my life and now I sleep on a dirty bag in the alley. Go figure. I'm Philip Meeker's only son, and look at me. I work at the pool hall so I can go buy a cut-rate burger on bargain day at the greasy spoon. So what are you doing here, kid?"

"I had some problems with your father just before he was attacked, and now the police are questioning me about it. I thought maybe you might know who would hate your father enough to try to kill him," Oscar said.

Brian laughed. "There's a long line, man. And I'm leading the parade. I might've gone over there and brained him myself with this pool cue or maybe a baseball bat. But I didn't have the nerve.

Worst I could do is smash the windows in his car," he said.

"I don't get along all that good with my dad either," Oscar said. "But I don't hate him. It seems like your dad was at least there for you. My dad wasn't there for us."

"Yeah, he was there for me all right," Brian sneered. "He was pushing 24–7. He never quit. He was after me to do my homework, to do every report just right. It got so I couldn't hack it anymore, and we fought. I got along okay with my mom because she didn't care what I was doing. Finally I figured the best revenge was to flunk out of school." A terrible smile twisted the young man's face. "I got even with him all right, but then I figured out I really did it to myself too. I thought I could stick it to him, but I'm paying the price . . . "

"You haven't seen your father in a long time, huh?" Oscar asked.

Brian wielded the cue again, slashing at the air. "Not since that night, dude. Not since then," he cried.

Brian's laughter followed Oscar out of the pool hall. Oscar figured Brian wasn't the one who attacked Phil Meeker. Brian was just a weak loser. He was right when he said he didn't have the nerve to take on his father.

"What do you think?" Oscar asked Danny as they drove off.

"Another dead end," Danny said.

"Yeah, the guy was just pathetic," Oscar said.

"You know, *hermano*," Danny said, "you're trying to make sense out of what happened to Mr. Meeker. You're looking for motives and logical stuff. Probably there's no reason why any of this happened. Meeker was just at the wrong place at the wrong time."

....

Oscar tried to put the incident from his mind over the next few days. He tried to concentrate on his classes and his friends. On Wednesday, a long-term substitute teacher was assigned to English. He was a middle-aged black man who seemed to know his stuff. Mr. Hand was even tougher than Meeker had been. And then, to everyone's surprise, a substitute teacher appeared in Ms. Windermere's biology class too. The sub did not say where Ms. Windermere was. But after class Oscar found Sandy Bailey, Ms. Windermere's niece. Sandy said, "She had an accident."

Oscar was shocked. "She's okay, isn't she? She wasn't hurt bad, was she?" He didn't want anything to have happened to his favorite teacher.

"She's all right," Sandy said, but she had a strange look on her face. Oscar had the feeling there was more to the story than Sandy was sharing. "She, uh . . . took a bad fall. But she's going to be okay."

Another fall? Oscar was alarmed. Ms. Windermere was a young woman. What was she falling all the time for? What was going on?

"Sandy, tell her we're all worried about her and she should take care of herself," Oscar said.

"I will," Sandy said, hurrying off.

"You remember last week when Ms. Windermere came to class all bruised and said she fell?" Oscar asked Danny.

"Yeah," Danny said. "She said she fell down hiking or something. Maybe she's got some sickness that makes her lose her balance or something."

"But, you know, I'm thinking maybe somebody hurt her that other time and now too," Oscar said darkly.

"Yeah," Danny said, "when some women get beat up, they invent all kinds of fake stories because they're embarrassed or they don't want to make trouble for the dude who did it. It's hard to believe Ms. Windermere is married to somebody who'd beat her, though. I've seen her husband, and he looks like a professional. He's a suit, man."

"I've heard that all kinds of guys beat their wives, not just guys who do rough jobs and don't make much money. Like some guys with college degrees kill their wives," Oscar said.

Oscar was sick to his stomach at the thought that Ms. Windermere might be hiding such a terrible secret. She had a master's degree, and she was going for more education. She lived in a beautiful home and came from a nice part of town. She was a beautiful, wonderful lady, smart and compassionate. Would she be dumb enough to put up with abuse from a man?

After school, Danny and Oscar went over to the neighborhood where Ms. Windermere lived. One Saturday evening she'd had her whole class over to look through telescopes, so they knew where she lived. Her house was on a hill, and she had friends who were astronomy buffs. They all brought telescopes and aimed them at the comet that had recently been discovered streaking through the sky. Oscar had vivid memories of not only seeing the comet with its long, fuzzy tail, but also seeing the rings of Saturn for the first time in his life. Then Ms. Windermere served cookies and apple cider to everybody.

Danny drove up to the Spanish style two-story home with the red-barrel-tile roof where Ms. Windermere lived. Both boys went to the door, and Oscar rang the bell.

When nobody answered, Oscar shouted, "You in there, Ms. Windermere?"

"Maybe she's in the hospital," Danny suggested.

"Look, all the blinds are shut," Oscar said, seeing that as an ominous sign.

Maybe Ms. Windermere was lying in the house badly injured and needing help.

"Hold it, dude," Danny said, "there's somebody at the window."

"Ms. Windermere, are you okay?" Oscar shouted at the figure behind the slightly tilted blinds.

"Yes, I'm fine," Ms. Windermere said. "Just a little bruised up. Me and my rock climbing. I should be old enough to know better. Did you boys come all the way over here to check on me?"

"Yeah, we were worried," Oscar said. "You sure you're okay?"

"I'm just a little sore. But, really, it was so sweet of you to come over. I'd ask you in, but I look a mess . . . I'll see you in a few days, boys, and be sure to be nice to your substitute teacher," Ms. Windermere said.

As Oscar and Danny returned to the truck, Oscar said, "I'm not so sure she fell down hiking."

"Maybe not, but if that's her story, what can we do, dude? If she won't blow the whistle on her husband then it's over, you hear what I'm saying?" Danny said.

"I'm going to talk to her niece tomorrow," Oscar said. "I'm going to try to get the truth from Sandy. Sandy's mom must be Ms. Windermere's sister . . . they've got to care what's happening to their family."

....

At school the next morning, before classes started, Oscar confronted Sandy. She was talking to some friends in front of the freshman algebra classroom.

"Sandy, we went to see your aunt yesterday," Oscar said. "She wouldn't show herself. She's bruised up real bad, I guess. How did that really happen?"

Sandy's became agitated. "Oh, she fell or something. I don't know," she stammered.

"Is your mom her sister?" Oscar asked.

"Yeah," Sandy said.

"Ms. Windermere is getting beat up by somebody, isn't she?" Oscar asked bluntly, hoping to shock Sandy into telling the truth. "I thought that the last time when she came to class all bruised and swollen."

"No, I mean, I don't know anything about it. Uh . . . Aunt Lisa is a very private person. She doesn't talk about stuff. My mom tried to . . . you know, talk about stuff, but Aunt Lisa clammed up," Sandy said.

"Look, Sandy, if a guy beat her up that badly then maybe next time he'll put her in the hospital or kill her. That's what happens when things like this just keep going," Oscar said. "He's dangerous, and somebody has to step in."

Several other students had gathered to listen. Oscar knew Ms. Windermere would hate being the focus of all this, but it couldn't be kept a secret anymore.

"Sandy, your aunt is the nicest, best teacher I've ever had. She's a really good person, and we all care about her. She doesn't deserve what's happening to her," Oscar said.

"She's no angel," Lindy Paul said. Lindy had come up in the midst of the conversation. Whenever some interesting conversation was taking place anywhere on campus, Lindy appeared, like ants at a picnic. "I mean, she's really sweet on the surface and everything, but she's not the good person you think she is, Oscar."

Oscar turned and glared at Lindy. "You don't know what you're talking about. Why don't you stop with the gossiping, Lindy? Haven't you done enough harm? What does it take to close that evil mouth of yours?" he snapped.

"Well," Lindy said, relishing the gossip she was about to divulge, almost as if she could taste it like the gooeyest, most delicious chocolate on her lips. "One time a friend of mine was passing the faculty lounge, and she happened to see Ms. Windermere getting real cozy with Mr. Meeker. Well, she's married right? Should Ms. Windermere be in the arms of this guy teacher like that?"

Oscar remembered Ms. Windermere telling him how once when she'd had personal problems, Mr. Meeker's concern had helped her out. Could she have been sharing her problem with Mr. Meeker and could he have given her a hug like any caring person might? Could Lindy and her nasty little friends have built that innocent gesture of compassion into something sordid? After all, Mr. Meeker could have been Ms. Windermere's father. He may well have felt fatherly toward her.

Oscar's attention was suddenly distracted as Sandy broke into convulsive sobs. She turned and ran as fast as she could around the corner of the building.

9 OSCAR TOOK OFF AFTER SANDY.
"Dude," Danny yelled after him,
"our class starts in two minutes.
Where are you running off to?"

Oscar didn't care about being late to
class now. He had to find Sandy and find
out what was really going on with her
aunt. But Sandy was nowhere to be seen.

Later, Oscar heard that Sandy had gone
to the office and said she was sick. Her
parents were called to come and pick
her up.

Oscar reluctantly sat through his
classes that day. He felt helpless about
everything. He couldn't clear his own
name from the suspicions swirling around
him about Mr. Meeker's attack. He
couldn't help Ms. Windermere even
though he was almost sure she was in
deep trouble.

Mr. Hand, the new English teacher,
launched into a vigorous discussion of
Thomas Wolfe's "The Lost Boy." Oscar had

read the story the night before, but he wasn't concentrating. Ever since Mr. Meeker had been attacked, he couldn't really focus on anything but that.

Mr. Hand talked about the story, then asked for comments.

"Things happen and we can't control them," Tina said.

"Yes," Mr. Hand said, "and the boy, Grover, is a symbol of something for the other young fellow, Eugene. What would that be? Oscar, what do you think?"

Oscar was jarred to attention at the mention of his name. "Eugene was looking for the house where his brother died. He was sort of looking for Grover, his lost brother. But I guess he was really looking for himself and his lost childhood," he said.

A smile split Mr. Hand's dark face. "Exactly!" he almost shouted.

The teacher seemed so happy with Oscar's reply, glad that a student had grasped the meaning of the story. Oscar was a good student. English was never his favorite subject, but he tried hard in every class. That's why Mr. Meeker's hostility and hassling had been so hard to take.

Now Oscar understood why all that had happened, but it was too late. Lindy had done her damage, like some vile bacteria entering the body and manifesting itself when the disease was incurable. Oscar could not repair the past that her gossip had poisoned.

Oscar liked Mr. Hand. The more he got to know him, the better he liked him. Oscar hated to say it, even just in his own mind, but it was so much better with Mr. Meeker gone. It was such an improvement. But, of course he was not glad about the way that it had happened.

About seven minutes before the end of the last class of the day, the public address system came on. Maryjane Hopkins, the principal, was going to address the students of Pico High School. It was common for her to make announcements, but she rarely broke into a class period like this. Ms. Hopkins' somber voice came over the PA system:

"It saddens me very much to announce to the students of Pico High School that our much-respected English teacher,

Mr. Philip Meeker, has died of injuries sustained during the attack on him. The attack on Mr. Meeker was a terrible shock to all of us, and we, students and staff alike, hoped for a good outcome. Now our community here extends to the family and friends of Mr. Meeker our deepest sympathies. Out of respect for Mr. Meeker we shall exit the school in silence. Tomorrow classes will be as usual, but grief counselors will be on campus for anyone who needs to talk to someone."

Oscar and Danny were walking out together as the flag was lowered to half-staff.

As they left the campus, Oscar said in a choked voice, "I didn't think the guy would die . . . I thought he'd recover and maybe even come back. I thought I'd maybe get the chance to tell him it wasn't me who lied about him."

"I guess if he'd have lived, he would've been like disabled and stuff, stuck in one of those nursing homes with tubes in him," Danny said. "Like my *abuela* would say, it was a favor from God that he died."

"Yeah," Oscar said, "but now it's

murder, and some people think I did it. You know how that makes me feel?"

"Now that it's a murder case, the police will work twice as hard. They'll probably get the guy now," Danny said.

"I bet Ms. Windermere will feel bad," Oscar said suddenly. "She liked the guy. He meant something to her because he was kind to her. Man, I wish I could talk to Ms. Windermere right now. I know she could make me feel better."

Just before Danny turned off on his street he grasped Oscar's shoulder and said, "Take it easy, man."

Oscar's mom was home when he walked in. She had worked the day shift.

"You heard, Oscar?" she asked, grim-faced.

"Yeah. They announced it at school," Oscar said.

"He never woke up. The poor man never woke up," his mom said. "He never had anything to say. Oh, Oscar, I am so afraid for you. I am worried they will think you were the one who attacked him."

"No, they won't think that," Oscar said

without conviction.

At 8:00, the phone rang at the Quintero house. Oscar's mom answered it.

"You don't know me," a woman opened in a high-pitched voice, "but my daughter is Sandy Bailey. She's a freshman at Pico High where your son goes. I have never had any problems with Sandy, but now she has run away. I was called to pick her up at school today, and she wasn't there when I got there. I've talked to all of her friends, and I was told she had a confrontation with your son right before she disappeared. The last anyone saw of her was when she was running across the school campus with your son pursuing her."

"I don't understand," Oscar's mom stammered. "My son has never mentioned a girl named Sandy Bailey."

Oscar's mom called out, "Oscar, come here quickly. There is a woman on the phone who says she is the mother of a Sandy Bailey who has run away after having a fight with you."

Oscar took the phone from his mother. "Mrs. Bailey? This is Oscar Quintero."

"You are the boy they questioned after the attack on the English teacher, aren't you?" Mrs. Bailey said in an accusing voice. "My daughter told me all about that. And now you were fighting with my girl, and she has disappeared. I want you to tell me the truth about what you know about my daughter's disappearance. My husband and I are distraught. Do you know where she is?"

"Mrs. Bailey, is Lisa Windermere your sister?" Oscar asked before he answered her question.

"Yes, but what has that got to do with what has happened to my daughter?" Mrs. Bailey said shrilly. "My little girl is missing! She has never run away like this before. Do you know where she is? If you do, you'd better tell me right now."

"I don't know where she is, Mrs. Bailey. Sandy and a bunch of us were talking about your sister, Ms. Windermere, getting all busted up. She's our favorite teacher, and we're all worried. All of a sudden, Sandy started crying, and she ran. I tried to catch up to her to find out what she was crying about, but I couldn't find her.

That's the last I saw of her," Oscar said.

"I think you might have caught up to her, young man," Mrs. Bailey said coldly. "I think you may very well have caught up to her and argued with her and perhaps hurt her like you hurt Mr. Meeker. I want you to tell me what has happened to my daughter, or I shall be calling the police!"

"I never saw your daughter after she ran away," Oscar said.

"I don't believe you. I think you are a very dangerous boy, and you know what has happened to our little girl," Mrs. Bailey said. "I hope to heaven Sandy is all right. We have no choice, my husband and I, but to call the police and report our suspicions." With that she hung up the phone.

Oscar told his mother about the bruises on Ms. Windermere and his suspicions that her husband was beating her. He explained what had happened at school.

"Oh, Oscar, now that woman is calling the police and accusing you of having something to do with her daughter's disappearance! You are getting in deeper and deeper. Lord help us!" his mom said.

"Mom, I need to go to Ms. Windermere's house and talk to her right away," Oscar said.

"I'll drive you," his mom said. "Come on. Come quickly. I'll do anything if you think it will help."

At 8:30 Oscar and his mother drove to the neighborhood where the Windermeres lived.

"There's her house, the one on the hill," Oscar said.

Oscar's mom pulled into the driveway. "Do you want me to go with you, Oscar?" his mom asked.

"No. I'll knock on the door and try to rouse Ms. Windermere. Maybe she'll let me in. Then I'll call you, Mom, and we can both go in. If she's really hurting and confused, you could help her make the right decision," Oscar said.

Oscar rang the bell, and then he pounded on the door. There was no answer. He shouted for Ms. Windermere, but there was no response. He walked around the side of the house, peering in the windows to see if anybody was home. The blinds were shut.

Fear coursed through Oscar's heart.

Maybe her husband had come home, and there was another, even more violent, argument. Maybe he had beaten her again. Maybe she was lying in the house too badly injured to call for help. Maybe she was dead in that silent house.

As Oscar was rounding the back of the house and going up the other side, he passed a utility shed. He stopped when he heard sobbing coming from inside the shed.

Oscar went to the shed and pushed open the sliding metal door.

"Sandy!" Oscar gasped, seeing the girl crumpled up in the corner by the rakes and shovels, sobbing.

"It's all my fault," Sandy cried, her shoulders shaking violently. "It's all my fault. *Everything*! I killed Mr. Meeker, and now I've killed Aunt Lisa too . . . I wish I was dead! I don't deserve to live!"

Oscar reached down and gently pulled the girl to her feet. "What are you talking about?" he asked.

Sandy collapsed in Oscar's arms, crying convulsively.

10

OSCAR TOOK SANDY to his mother, and she helped her into the backseat of the car. Oscar's mom called the Baileys on her cell phone.

"This is Mrs. Quintero, Oscar's mother," she said.

Before she could say any more, Mrs. Bailey cut in. "The police are on their way to your house, Mrs. Quintero. I've told them that I suspect your son of kidnapping our daughter and harming her. I've told them . . ."

"Please shut up for a minute," Oscar's mom said with sudden strength in her voice. "Your daughter is here with us at your sister's home, at Ms. Windermere's. Your girl is very upset, but she is all right. She was hiding in the toolshed of her aunt's house when we found her."

Mrs. Bailey seemed stunned. She said nothing for a long moment. Then she said, "I'll call the police and tell them to meet us there." With that she hung up.

"Sandy," Oscar asked softly, "what did you mean that you killed Mr. Meeker? You didn't kill anybody. You didn't hurt your aunt, either."

"I did . . . I killed Mr. Meeker . . . I heard about him dying, and it's my fault. I yelled and screamed for my aunt, but she didn't answer. She must be dead in that house, and it's all because of me," Sandy sobbed.

Oscar's mom took the phone again, and this time she dialed 911. "There is a woman in a house who may be hurt and in need of help. We don't know for sure if she is injured, but she may have been beaten unconscious so she can't come to the door," Oscar's mom said, giving the address of the Windermere house.

"He beats her all the time," Sandy cried. "He's a demon. Nobody he works with would believe it. He's so charming. And then he drinks, and he's a monster!"

"Ms. Windermere's husband?" Oscar asked.

Sandy nodded. "He programs computers . . . he's some kind of genius. He makes good money, and he's hot-looking, and Aunt Lisa was crazy about him. But everybody saw how jealous he was. If she just looked at another guy on the street, he made her life miserable," Sandy said between sobs. She kept wiping her eyes and blowing her nose. "He started hitting her really bad when he . . . found out . . ." The tears came in a torrent again, running down the girl's face. "Oh, it's my fault. That junior, Lindy Paul, she was going on about Ms. Windermere hugging some guy and how she's married and it was Mr. Meeker and they must be having a romance and . . . I called Aunt Lisa. I told her what they were saying. I didn't know . . . I didn't know." She was crying so violently, she couldn't finish the sentence.

"Take it easy, Sandy," Oscar said. "What didn't you know?"

"That . . . that *he* was on the extension . . . Jack, her husband. He heard everything I said. Don't you see how it was my fault? I called Aunt Lisa and told her what Lindy Paul was saying, and that started everything . . . Jack went into a terrible rage and hurt her. And it wasn't even true what Lindy said. Mr. Meeker was just giving my aunt a hug like a brother would," Sandy said.

Oscar's mom put her arms around the girl, stroking her hair. "It wasn't your fault. You didn't know what would happen, *niña*," his mom said.

"Do you think Jack killed Mr. Meeker?" Oscar asked.

"Aunt Lisa was so afraid it was him, but she didn't want to believe it. He played golf, and she found this busted golf club a few days after the attack . . . there was stuff on it, like blood. But Aunt Lisa loved him so much, she didn't want to believe it," Sandy said.

The police arrived minutes after the paramedics. After briefly talking to Oscar and his mother, the police broke into the Windermere house.

Minutes after that, a black BMW pulled into the driveway. A young man jumped out. He was casually dressed and very handsome. Seeing all the emergency vehicles, he became alarmed. "This is my house," he shouted. "What's going on here? Where's my wife? Has something happened to Lisa?"

"Sir," one of the police officers said, restraining Mr. Windermere from entering the house. "You'd better let us check things out first. The paramedics have gone in. We have a report there might be a lady hurt in there."

"My wife!" the man said in a loud voice. "Was there a robbery? She was fine when I left for work this morning. Oh, man, what happened?"

The Baileys pulled up then, and Sandy jumped from the Quintero car and ran into the arms of her parents. Oscar heard her telling her story between hysterical sobs.

"He hurt Aunt Lisa! I think he killed Mr. Meeker too. And it's all my fault. I carried that horrible gossip about Aunt Lisa, and he heard it. It's my fault Mr. Meeker is dead, and maybe he's killed Aunt Lisa too!" Sandy cried.

"Shhhh," Mrs. Bailey said, holding her daughter in her arms. "It's not your fault. It's nobody's fault but his. I told her a hundred times to leave him, but she wouldn't."

The paramedics carried Lisa Windermere out on a gurney. She was lying still with her head bandaged. She was receiving oxygen as they wheeled her toward the ambulance. Jack Windermere tried to break free of the police and go to her. "I've got to be with her," he said. "That's my wife! I need to be with her!"

Two police officers restrained the man.

"The paramedics will take good care of your wife, sir," one of the officers said. "We need for you to come downtown with us and answer a few questions. You might want a lawyer."

Sandy yelled as Mr. Windermere went by with the police. "He did it! He beat her up like that! He did it all the time. He's a monster. I think he killed Mr. Meeker too! Aunt Lisa told me about a bloody golf club in the garage. Maybe he's gotten rid of it by now."

Lisa Windermere was taken to Community General Hospital and admitted into intensive care. She had suffered a brain concussion and fractured skull along with several rib fractures. Her face was a mass of cuts and bruises. Some of the bruises were a few days old, and some had obviously been inflicted that morning.

Jack Windermere kept telling the police that an intruder must have broken into the home and injured his wife. He said that when she regained consciousness, she would tell them that he was innocent. He said he loved his wife dearly. He kept saying that, over and over.

For 12 hours Lisa Windermere was too weak to be questioned. But when she had recovered enough strength to talk to the police, she told them that her husband had spent half the night beating her, with fists and a wooden rod. She said he had hurt her before but never like this. And then she told the police where her husband probably disposed of the bloody golf club, which was found buried in the Windermere's cactus garden. Three days later Jack Windermere was arrested on charges of murder and assault with intent to commit murder.

....

Oscar Quintero and many of his fellow students from Pico attended the funeral of Philip Meeker—a small, sad affair with only the brother and his ex-wife representing the family.

Things returned to normal at Pico High School, and Oscar Quintero got on well with the new English teacher, Mr. Hand, and the new biology teacher, Ms. Sanchez. Oscar heard several months later that Ms. Windermere had returned to teaching biology at another high school. He was glad that she had recovered. He envied her new students. He remembered her every time he looked up at the stars and every time he thought about his future career in science. And wherever that career took him, Oscar knew he would owe it to the brief, shining time Lisa Windermere had touched his life so profoundly.